The Land Of Hidden Thoughts

Saidou DM Camara
(Gainako Poet)

Ukiyoto Publishing

All global publishing rights are held by

Ukiyoto Publishing

Published in 2022

Content Copyright © Saidou DM Camara
(Gainako Poet)
ISBN 9789360161828

All rights reserved.

No part of this publication may be reproduced, transmitted, or stored in a retrieval system, in any form by any means, electronic, mechanical, photocopying, recording or otherwise, without the prior permission of the publisher.

The moral rights of the author have been asserted.

This is a work of fiction. Names, characters, businesses, places, events, locales, and incidents are either the products of the author's imagination or used in a fictitious manner. Any resemblance to actual persons, living or dead, or actual events is purely coincidental.

This book is sold subject to the condition that it shall not by way of trade or otherwise, be lent, resold, hired out or otherwise circulated, without the publisher's prior consent, in any form of binding or cover other than that in which it is published.

This book is entirely dedicated to my beloved Mum Marie Ayo Jallow

Acknowledgement

First of all, I would like to recognize the blessings of the Omniscient, the Omnipotent and the Omnipresent- Allah (S.W.T). I was able to fill the blank pages of my book because of his wills. Therefore, I am returning gratitude to whom gratitude emanates from.

My sincere gratitude and appreciation go to my beautiful and benevolent parents who accorded me my fundamental right to education. I am praying for them all and sundry for long life in order to benefit from my financial fruits of education.

I cannot express enough thanks to the following people who in one way or other contributed immensely to completion of the book: My dad, Dawda Fatou Camara, mum Marie Ayo Jallow. My aunties, Mai Bah, Jarrie Ceesay, Fatou Bojang Jallow Huray Camara and of course my siblings, Hawa Camara, Omar Camara, Essa Camara, Sainey Camara, Gibbie Camara, Amie Camara, Yassin Camara, Saikou Camara, Fatou Camara, Halimatou Camara Bintou Camara and the entire Camara Kunda for their endless support.

I will be very ungrateful if I don't recognize the efforts of my mentor, a brother, uncle, teacher and a friend Alhagie Njie (Malcom X Jr) without the help of Mr. Njie my dream of becoming an author would have been aborted. The first person to introduce me to the world of literature, I'm highly indebt to him for his professes, and high sense of humor. His legacies shall forever live.

I won't do justice to myself without thanking these special people in my life, they play one of the most crucial role in my life, ModouLamin Sowe, one of the strongest pillars in my life a brother, teacher, friend, mentor and a director, CEO and Director of Young Stars Movie Production. Mr. Adama Minteh, a friend, teacher and a brother the Production Manager of Young Stars Movie Production and then to my late aunty Ya-Kumba Keita (RIP) of Brusubi, a phenomenal woman whose kindness and love for humanity knows no boundary. Mr. Ousainou Jonga I see you, humble and trustworthy brother you are, thank you making me explore my limits.

Special recognition and appreciations of efforts goes to Lady Chilel Secka

Am eternally grateful to her, she has been constantly there for me. Without her completing this book won't have been possible. Thank for the typing and proof reading.

I am highly indebted to the following people for their utmost understanding and encouragement they invested on me when I embarked on this crucial journey in my education Edrisa Jallow, Ebrima Njie, Ndumbeh Secka, Alex A Manneh and the entire staff and students of Brusubi Upper and Senior Secondary School. My special recognition of efforts goes to Mr. Jaiteh. Head of

Language department of Brusubi Senior Secondary School. And to my able principal Mr. Peter O Jatta.

Of course to my erudite brother Bakery Bah, I am profoundly grateful to you. Thank you all for your endless support since day one.

And then to my learned brother and friend Baisru Jallow alias Legal Hustler. You made me believed in myself when I needed it the most. Without a doubt this book is published because of you. Thank you for the inspirations and proof read

About The Book

"The Land of Hidden Thoughts" is a florilegium that fosters stopgap, highlights potential powers and forces that are decelerating black societies from redemption, reintegration, independence, and black supremacy. It fills the lyrical soul with a craving for regard to great and deep expression. The nectar that spills from the mug of genius imbues and delights, leaving mediocrities inebriated with admiration and esteem.

In addition, the book shed lights on societal patrimonies which are verbal treasure troves of countless mitigations for various greats who have lifted us to thrilling heights but have been silenced by true minatory forces.

Intro Verse

"…for greatness and grandiloquence in this, our adored art, revolving around missing pieces of earthen secrets,

Finding my roots, embracing echoes in past-painting palette,

Living in the shadow of darkness as silver tears

Restoring millions of lost legacies and untold stories of greatness,

Welcome to the land of hidden thoughts…"

Contents

League Of Assassins	1
The Dark Pen	3
The Unheard Cry	5
The Love In Vain	10
Free The System	12
The Devil's Thrones	15
Islamic Phobia	17
The Words Of My Mum	19
I Am A Proud Africanist	21
Fight With Purpose	23
Letter To Mr President	25
The Pain	27
I Cry For Gambia	29
Shadows Of Exile	33
Professional Drunkard	35
Fractures	38
Back To Africa	41
The Lost Legacies	45
Home, As I Remember It	46
Ode Of Riddle	49
Echoe Voices Of Mother Africa	51
Men Don't Cry	54
The Undesired Child	57

He Don't Deserve Your Cry	60
The Art Of Smoking	62
Letter To My Future Wife	63
Poetry	65
Finding Peace In A World Of Conflict	67
For The Gone	69
Black Widow	71
A Morning Walk Along The Beach	73
Phases Of Character	75
Village Play	77
Invisible Quivering	79
My Unborn Child	80
The Immotal Love	82
My Phoneminal Lady	84
From The Ruins	86
Africa In Shackles	88
The Negro	91
Double-Faced	93
Drought	95
My Grandmother	97
About the Author	*100*

League Of Assassins

In a nation brimming of assaults! Façades!
Fallen victims of language and power abuses
Swore allegiance for righteousness
In reality unending darkness widespread
Their real meaning hidden beneath the settlements of
ceremonies of lies and falsehood
Hospitals turn into institutional graveyards
Innocent beings used as experimental specimens
Endless justices denial
Murders celebrated as hero
Cleansing only archive by fire.

The price of existence is half the cost of a cabbage
the price of talking the reality bounce cost your head.
Infamy is what they inquire
and indoctrination's what they spread
Walking freely with innocent blood on their hands!
Hidden realities, spotted lines, ain't never marked
In an experience that is to say adequate of facades
Where if you talk, you receive captured to a cross

We have seen blessings buried beneath blunt
blunders
Several intellectuals giants strolled into silence
We have seen monsters roars in wild

The Land Of Hidden Thoughts

Through depths and dunes in dungeons
Through thick and thin, we trudge across dark streams
Before the sun rises, we have walked the wildness
Until dreams are fulfilled, missions accomplished, peace is restored, our safety restored, there shall be no recess
Until we modulate, there shall be no reasonable reason to resting
We sleep and wave, before endure regret
Ministers with swords beneath their smiles
Laceration of sinister spikes
Foul fragrance of familiar foes
Secretly they did us woes
A brutal butcher's knife in Thor tongues
Their betrayal is no more a surprise
Our hopes remain rumpled feather
When shall Justice be served ??

The Dark Pen

As a vessel of wisdom and power
The feckless and unctuous exploits
And abuses my power
As they sit in the comfort of their zone
With dozens of white papers and double-edged sphering swords

I bleed so much that no one comes to my rescue
Been in love with all levels of industries and Government
They use me to victimize the innocent
They use me to corrupt the uncorrupt
To justify the injustice
I am the dark pen

I am the dark pen
Fear me, for I am more powerful
Then the most powerful army in the World
Severer than the deadliest pandemic
I am more dangerous than the
Most deadly Vernon in the world
My ink is the most dangerous poison
I am the dark pen
I am the broken hope

Obsequious to my holder accordingly,
I am the stock house of influence and power
Facilitating and promoting invention and innovation
Convictions and conventions
Influence and affluence

The earthquakes of destructions I causes
Tsunamis of hopes I break
Volcanic eruptions of genocides I cause
I am the dark one

The Unheard Cry

Life has become a dirge,
Torn image,
Frustration in the content of epilation
Silence has engulfed my life
So, entangled in melancholy
Decade passed,
As if a century I've gone through,
With your memories,
Still waiting for you,

Vividly I remember those days,
When you used to kiss my forehead
You used to give me "saliboo" on every "Eid"
Perhaps I live on,
By rejoicing those moments
Somebody takes me to my love

The Land Of Hidden Thoughts

In an unending wait, I'm
Which has made me?
A living corpse alike…
Since when you disappeared,
Never have I wore ornaments,
Never have I prettified myself
As for you only,
My beauty has life….

I become mute and glossily
Whenever our child asks me about you
Without you,
Everything seems gloomy
As if,
Flowers have lost their bloom
Wind is the same, without breeze
So are mounts, without serenity

I see no change,
In any motion of sun
I feel no warmth,
In any moment now
And no harmony I've,

Without you, my love
No peace comes to my door

Do you forget your promise?
Of never leaving me alone!
How can you leave me?
Our souls lived together!
Have you forgotten that too?

Always I pray for you,
In twilights
On the door, I always stare,
For you may come,
Never my eyes blink,

Except quivering soul,
I've nothing,
Not even tears also!!
Day and night, I go by mourning
From every side,
Sleepless nights I always observe,
Since when you disappear
Nightmares have surrounded me,

You're alive, in my heart
Come back, O' my crown
Without you,
Irrelevant and aimless,
My existence serves
I hear no bird chirping
I see every tree mourning
After when you disappeared
As if I had rendezvous with any calamity

For you,
I've renounced this world
Like every saint,
Now every stranger knows me
As in search of you,
I walk miles every day
Since when you disappeared!!

Insane I've become,
For your single countenance
So also, I crave for our reunion
I talk gibberish, I'm deranged,

People comment about me
What's its reason?
Only you who know
O' my confidant
My shrieks are calling you
Till we reunite

The Love In Vain

Love is a fire that burns the unseen,
A wound that aches yet isn't felt,
And always discontent contentment,
A pain that rages without hurting,

A longing for nothing but to long,
A loneliness in the midst of people,
A never feeling pleased when pleased,
A passion that gains when lost in thought.

It's being enslaved of your own free will;
It's counting your defeat in victory;
It's staying loyal to your killer.

But if it's so self-contradictory,
How can love be love when love chooses?
Bring human hearts into sympathy?

Love is a fire that burns the unseen,
A wound that aches yet isn't felt,
An always discontent contentment,
A pain that rages without hurting,

A longing for nothing but to long,
A loneliness in the midst of people,
A never feeling pleased when pleased,
A passion that gains when lost in thought.

It's being enslaved of your own free will;
It's counting your defeat in victory;
It's staying loyal to your killer.

Free The System

Living in a nation full of fear and terror
Tired of speaking because they are all the same
Tired of trying because they are all the same
This is beyond valuation!
Beyond forgery or imitation
Its hurts seeing young and innocent people losing their lives due to a lack of proper
And enough Health facilities, in the name of politics
But this what happen when you elect Lucifer as your leader
Soldiers of the Lucifer running the system
Until the end of time, we will keep on crying

We give you the way
As the moon gives way to the sun,
Forget your pride, we elected you
How dare you be on Twitter twittering
While your people are dying?

How dare you be flying overseas while your land is sinking?

ENOUGH IS ENOUGH

We won't keep on standing this while they kill us quietly

We don't have esteem for greedy politicians.

Won't you be ashamed to stand tomorrow and tell your children?

What you have done for this country?

Instead of sending the youth to school

You sending them to pool

The youth place is not in prison but at school, at workplaces

You sell our waters to the foreigners,

And our fishermen are still suffering from your actions

The police are supposed to protect us

Today they are the ones killing us

And our mothers will only have their eyes to cry when we die

Everybody is into this fight; we are the witnesses of these events

You should handle the prisons not our country

The presidential palace is the temple of the thieves

While our national jail is full of innocent lives

The National Assembly is the valley of demons,

A manufacturing ground for self-enrichment while the nation suffocates

You take us for corpses but mercenaries alone won't be enough

A grave could not hold back the living dead

Let it be clear: enough is enough

What to do with a country that is unable to develop?

You sold our oil, and we are the ones begging for water

You claim all our wealth for yourself and ran away

We have all types of degrees but can't manage to find a job

And if you are sick, it's a disaster: hospitals are at their lowest

Everything you take in people who have made your ancestors slaves become legal like "Auchan"

The Devil's Thrones

As I was on my feet in a courtroom feeling disgraceful and embarrassed amid the merciless army of Satan on my left, and the delegation of angels on my right. Satan as the attorney has in hand the records of my misdeeds concerning worldly affairs.

Seated on his throne chair handling a might stone in hand, I have no attorney to defend me on trials concerning my misdeeds presented in the courtroom. Such deeds include; dishonesty and hypocrisy, corruption and theft, fornication and adultery, and unlawful killings of innocent people. This marks the beginning of my persecution or hardship.

There was nothing I could say to save my skin from harm. All the evidence is right before Satan.

The merciless army of Satan smiled at my doom as tears rolled down my eyes. For they knew with certainty the hour of my downfall has come.

Behold!

A sudden presence of a bright light shining in the courtroom caused the smiling faces of the devil to turn into fear or being in a state of terror.

That sudden presence of light shining bright that night was none other than my small good deeds.

Darkness disappeared to give away.

And words of glorification were all the angels could utter.

Records of my misdeeds in the custody of Satan were set on fire.

Glory be to God, the most Gracious and the most Merciful.

Islamic Phobia

They never annoyed to state even individual lyrics of the Quran,

They never bother to state even individual units of the hadith

They were never annoyed to express even division of the Islamic fiqh

Nor do they always try to create genuine research about Islam

Yet they hold exploding and talking against Islam

Hilarious! How does an individual fight you about an entity they

Experience not about?

Merely bearing an extended beard, doesn't marry a subversive,

Nor does tiring that frightening dark dress

Do you care how many juveniles expire each era in Gaza?

How often Yemen, Jordan, or Syria, are damned?

How many public are expiring in Palestine continually?

Do you visualize it?

Do you feel it?

Do you learn it?

Do we scare you?

Our concepts are deep but available for understanding

For skilled lies a substance in the light

Those indicate on us completely crucifying destructively

The sharp and abhorrent shadows of mystery

In redefining the opinion of us as a country with its government

They mention the ineffective mind is the demon laboratory

See our standards as a human has existed spoiled and Tampere

No validity is going to be fine when

We probing blameworthy place

The Words Of My Mum

Dark quiet in the night
When everyone is as sleep
She wakes me up
Put me right on her arms
And said listen, my son
For I am about to tell you
Something that is going to be a
Spring board and a
A map for you in the
Rest of your life

She said in her most melodious and
Eloquent voice
The world will always be one step
Ahead of you
Every day pray to Lord and ask for
His blessing and mercy
Guidance and protection

Be dutiful to your parents
And always ask for their blessings
Respect and protect them
When they reach to old age
Provide for them and respect them
Never rise your voice on them

You are a reservoir of hope
An encyclopedia of knowledge
That must be passed and preserved for generations to come
You must never be used in the expense of money
Blinded by delusions and fancy of this world

Be vigilant and be wise
Be a truth teller not a truth seller
Be wise in speech
Respect the elders and show mercy to the young
Then the in the heaven shall have mercy on you
Feed the poor and help the able disable
Shelter the homeless and visit the sick
Protect the orphans and comfort the widows

I Am A Proud Africanist

I am a proud Africanist,

From the mama lands flowing with gold and diamonds, lands of my ancestors.

Embedded with beautiful and rich cultures

I am a proud Africanist,

I have built civilizations, toiled for nothing, and reaped the wind.

The struggle for survival runs in my veins

The spirit of patriotism highly articulated in my heart

I am a proud Africanist,

Others mistake me for a bigot, a slave, or a thankless brat.

But in actuality, I'm not

I'm the hope for Africa

The symbol of unity and love

The symbol of peace.

I am a proud Africanist,

I have birthed inventions, and my name is not associated with any.

I'm born to be a ruler not be ruled

I am a proud Africanist

I am strong, daring, and fearless, and my veins drip with ripped marrows.

I am a proud Africanist,

My wisdom is in my color – dark, black and fits with any variance.

I am a proud Pan Africanist,

I am the hope of the world, I still treasure the jungle filled with greens.

I am a proud Pan Africanist,

My shape is a bottle; I treasure the rhythms of my protruding buttocks.

Dancing to the beautiful rhythms of the drums.

I am a proud Pan Africanist,

I speak with divine accents, feed with the roles of nature, and sleep free.

Beautiful rivers and seas with fresh waters I live in

Fight With Purpose

Sometimes you need to the feel the pain and sting of defeat,
To excite the truthful love and purpose that God
Predestined inside of you.
Purpose is an essential determinant of you
It is the reason you are in this place sphere
At this particular of time

Purpose crosses discipline
Our very existence is wrapped
In our current fashion we are present to achieve
Whatever you pick for a career course
Remember the struggles in transit goal
Are only resources to shape you for your purpose.

When I dare to challenge the bureaucracy that would
Relegate us to martyrs and stereotypes following no
Clear archival cultures
No hopes of talents when I questioned

That order of treachery a differing course
Opened brave for me
The course to my destiny
When God has entity for you
It doesn't matter who stands against you

Today I'm not just a writer
I'm the spur of verses and stanzas of freedom fighters
Conquering the crumbling mountains and rotting ridges of doubts

I'm and not more a visionary
My aims are certain
I have been in the black hole
For far too long
Absorbing wholeness, outside admitting
My light and capacity to escape
But those days are over
You can administer accompanying future
And so, do you subsequently do I

Letter To Mr President

Dear Mr. President,
As I lift up my pen,
My heart is heavy,
My face is swollen,
And tears are rolling down my cheeks.
I can't just measure my unflinching sadness seeing you
And corrupt ministers dressed in academic regalia.

Dressing in all white and blue with your pockets deeply impregnated with citizens taxes,
Furiously gallivanting, craving to be address as honorable
When you are terrible horrible.

When the spirit and power of money overshadow weak minds, greedy and corrupted souls, corruption is given a breath.

Mr. President, we voted you with the hope for a better change,

Instead you are driving from worse to worst.

We voted you with the hope you could dream in reality

And lead us to the promise land,

Instead, you are sluggish and slumbering in daydreams.

Dear Mr. President,

Our education system has been corrupted to the core,

Lack of enough facilities in the system,

Students are like poor refuges in refugee camps.

Their needs aren't met,

In the end, many of them lose consciousness

And move onto sell their integrity and honesty for a little or no gain.

We live in a Gambia where the respect for human rights is just put in a paper.

Citizens' lives are at risks,

Too much of killings innocent souls.

Mr. President, security reinforcement is a public demand.

Rethink your actions and do the right thing because the future is keenly watching with us.

The Pain

Deep down I am sad and feeling the gloom,
But wearing a smiley face and hiding my pain.
Why did we part our ways?
I can't get through,
I can't control my tears, but it's in vain.

Don't tell me to stop,
I won't be able to,
I can't express my pain in any other form.
All the games of love and blame,
It's not surreal,
It's not the same.
I have emotions and feel a lot,
Please think once more,
Please give it a thought.

Sitting in this oblivion of my mind,
I feel the emptiness creeping inside of me.

Forsaking my sanity over these memories,
I ought to work on my sanity,
For this broken heart may not be mended,
Yet, my love for you seems never to end
No matter how hard I try.

Half love is vanity,

My heart ripped off facing the giant waves of the Ocean of bitterness.

Standing at the shore getting a glimpse of every broken memory we had.

I Cry For Gambia

Cochlea catches our skyrocketed profuse wails,
Spinning in firmament like the dusk dust mosaic,
For we are the lost quaking sphere's denizens,
Home of affluence splendid as dungeon of goal,
The sinking horizon of self-acclaimed blacks' giant.

My common sense has been abused but who really cares?
The smiling coast of Africa is sinking;
The smiling coast of Africa is crying;
The smiling coast of Africa is bleeding;
And no one seems to care.

At what point do we use our collective humanity?
Our streets are flooded with blood of innocent people,
Our homes fussed up with chaos and confusion,
Darkness and insecurity.

The sinking land of honey and colloquium flows,
Where helpless bees are of the fresh honey deprived,
By the grizzled lagoons and greedy guerillas surfing,
And aversive dragon blazing the helpless bees' hives,
Assassinating the hope of having a good morrow,
Jealousy and hearted ripping off the heart.

Innocent souls killed and buried, that which bring up
The roaring of the lion in the jungle
To play fast and desperate and lose the belt to Hare aftermath.

The welkin hearkens the echoes and voices,
Voices of the hissing intestines of the orphans,
The orphans of the drowning land in whose it trumpets,
Hungers pangs in the hollow bowels nocturnal and diurnal.

The Gambia has fallen into the dark realm,
With the drive of the bastardized bastards.
The Gambia has sunk into the dungeon of disaster,
In the hands of the clueless souls of no discernment,
Heaven upon you we call for revival mid survival!

And the government says sorry to this one tragedy,
The same sorry they said last week and week before last,
The same sorry they said last year and year before last.
I cry for you Gambia!

Corruption is our common ratio permutations,
Daily rhyme of our radios and televisions,
Flying papers are dark, broadcasts opaque,
Gloms descending on our roofs like woeful haggard.

I am just a voice speaking for the orphan left homeless,
I am the voice speaking for the communities,
I am the voice speaking for the voiceless,
But hey what will my one only voice do?
How far can I go alone?
But if I have God,
If I have your voice, their voices,
Then our voice will become the noise,
Our voice will become the voice of the people,
We will raise a shout, knock the guns and machetes.

Enough is enough!
Rest in peace to all the departed souls.

Shadows Of Exile

Locked in cages out of ranges
Shattered and battered
In my own hood I was traded
Enslaved and shipped across the Atlantic Ocean
A journey of no return
Harrowing and giggling in doom and gloom.
The firehouse writing in my arms
Threatening to rip them apart
All I have I wished was for it guzzle out gallons
To douse the flames and silence the scream

My tongue is glued
My ears fed, the negatives they wish
The sky above is blue
They sing dark tunes to my ears

They watch my life clothed with poverty
Sleepless nights and an empty stomach

Naked feet and a scorched scalp

My dreams they write off, am black and poor

Deaf ears are all I've been offered

Nobody stares to read on my face my frustrations

The sky speaks not of my voices to be heard

The wind blew off a smile, and a laughter I've turned to be

Another night another sleep, a hopeless dawn

Another laughter another wishes, a cruel world

Yet another being in me to be born, a smile yet to be born

Another light comes fear, a dumb one yet to find a kind ear

I ought for a lone cry, in the midst of silent jungle

Glance to the trees and plants, calm and green with no cries

A smile for a minute, next a thought of the night

Never to speak of the dreams as a poor child, I will write

A pen and a green leaf need no extra ear for my tongue.

Professional Drunkard

Too small yet so might
Gather around mates
You I pen words with
I have a confession to make
That not many of you know about me

I've been hiding this for far too long
But now I think that you should know
I'm a professional drunkard
Drowning daily in bottles

But don't be dismayed
For I mean not the bottle of wine
But that of words
In it I drown my sorrows and find my muse
Defuse my pain

I'm a workaholic
Yes, that's my confession
See, I'm not a poet
But a word addict
Addicted in adding values in people
Addicted in lyrics of alcoholics of academic's exercises

Like drunkards live for a bottle
So, do me for words
Inking is my drinking
Poetry is my favorite beer

I drink to drown my sorrows
I drink to exhibit my joy
I drink to speak for the voiceless
I drink to make someone smile
I drink to shake volumes
I drink to wink the eyes of the cowardice
For no coward sleep when I put my pen on paper

Dear mates
You I pen words with

Now you know what's being my secret
But before you go, I have this one request

One day if I sleep to no awake
Fill a bottle with words
And pour it on my grave
Then write on my tombstone these words:

Touch not this grave
With your pen less hands
For here lies under this part of the earth
A professional drunkard
Not of the bottle of wine
But that of words.

Fractures

In that fair capital where pleasure is crowned
Amidst her myriad courtiers, riots and rules,
I too have been a suitor.
Radiant eyes
Were my life warmth and sunshine, outspread arms
My gilded deep horizons,
I rejoiced!
In yielding to all amorous influence
And multiple impulsion of the flesh,
To feel within my being surge and sway
The force that all the stars acknowledge too.
Amid the nebulous humanity
Where I an atom crawled and cleaved and sundered,
I saw a million motions, but one law;
And from the city's splendor to my eyes
The vapors passed and there was naught but Love,
Ferment turbulent, intensely fair,
Where beauty beckoned and where Strength pursued.

There was a time when I thought much of fame,
    And laid the golden edifice to be
    That in the clear light of eternity
Should fitly house the glory of my name.

But swifter than my fingers pushed their plan,
    Over the fair foundation scarce begun,
    While I with lovers dallied in the sun,
The ivy clambered and the rose-vine ran.

And now, too late to see my vision, rise,
In place of golden pinnacles and towers,
Only some sunny mounds of leaves and flowers,
    Only beloved of birds and butterflies.

My friends were duped, my favored deceived;
    But sometimes, musing sorrowfully there,
    That flowered wreck has seemed to me so fair
    I scarce regret the temple unachieved

        For there were nights
        My love to him whose brow

Has glistened with the spoils of nights like those,
Home turning as a conqueror turns home,
What time green dawn down every street up rear
Arches of triumph!
He has drained as well
Joy's perfumed bowl and cried as I have cried:
Be fame their mistress whom Love passes by.
This only matter: from some flowery bed,
Laden with sweetness like a homing bee,
If one has known what bliss it is to come,
Bearing on hands and breast and laughing lips
The fragrance of his youth's dear rose. To him
The hills have bared their treasure, the far clouds
Unveiled the vision that o'er summer seas
Drew on his thirsting arms.
This last thing known,
He can court danger, laugh at perilous odds,
And, pillowed on a memory so sweet,
Unto oblivious eternity
Without regret yield his victorious soul,
The blessed pilgrim of a vow fulfilled.

Back To Africa

For long we've been crying,

Tears wetting and drying,

In a limbo of blacks being part of human race, I am left thinking.

The journey for survival in the diaspora is humiliating.

Living in the diaspora in a limbo,

Blacks suffering and standing still in akimbo.

See, for years...

For years we are a scapegoat, tortured and enslaved for over decades.

See

Ironically, I have one finger pointing on the whites and four on myself.

For my people promote plurality against unity

And corruption is against responsibility.

If coming together is our fear,

Then we shall perish as fools and sink in tear.

Racism,

I say, Racism is real, alive and kicking and its end is eternity.

For as long as we arrange humanity and humans into class,

Isolating the poor, disregarding the uneducated and uplifting the wealthy.

All these are happening here in my Africa.

We value not our identity, complaints are raining and solutions are draining.

Promises has conquered fulfillment,

Expectations has enslaved strives and blabbers has superseded action.

My thoughts of Africa's freedom can't put me to rest.

For my ability is put to grave by those in responsibility.

What has made us so fooled to define light from darkness?

The whites and blacks, both are humans,

But the heart feels not for the brain.

The tones of a zebra colored violins,

That produces song with its beautifully decorated black and white string, produces song that are enjoyed by all race.

Why are you in a haste to send me to my grave?
The protected abused are settled.
Plurality shall turn to unity.

A black man knows where he belongs,
He knows respect he won't gain in her sibling's territory.
Your refusals to return is squeezing your throats
Please come back and turn a new page.

For the beautiful wombs of tradition, culture, moral and respect has kept you a sit so return,
Return and never turn back.
The vast land of Africa's fertility and morality protects your sovereignty.

Why run away from the mother that gave you soul?
Africans,
I say, it's high time and the right time for us to realized our roles on earth.
Else destruction and exploitation shall ruin our dishes.
Our ancestors are angry,

Our way of living is less amalgamated and
incompatible to their time.

The blame game must end.

Responsibility has to be shouldered and embraced
without corruption, racism and favoritism.

Only then,

Only then shall Africa revolt with her revolutionaries
free and elated in all states and sites.

We must unite or perish as fools.

The Lost Legacies

What is Success? Out of the endless ore
Of deep desire to coin the utmost gold
Of passionate memory; to have lived so well
That the fifth moon, when it swims up once more
Through orchard boughs where mating orioles build

That soul partakes whose inspiration fills
The springtime and the depth of summer skies,
The rainbow and the clouds behind the hills,
That excellence in earth and air and sea
That makes things as they are the real divinity.

Gone when the night was gentle
Greater accomplishment but little known
The prophecies have come to live

It's hard to live up to these expectations

Home, As I Remember It

Home, as I remember it
I've seen the grandeur of the hills
All the cobblestones and clotheslines in Sare Janko

I've stood in bars and on bridges in Kerr Batch
I've tasted fresh citrus in Chamen
And I'll be up Sare Alpha soon

But somewhere deep down in light
I think and I hope that I'll always be inclined
Toward "that peninsula where the sun doth shine"

Where children come to know the world
With cool grass between their toes
Chanting melodies of greatness

Surrounded by the balmy heat of the shinning Sun
Balancing carefully a plate prepared by several pairs

Of weathered freckled hands

A plate laden with the manifestations of recipes passed down like

A mother's maiden name to a firstborn son

The heat is interrupted only intermittently by a cool breeze

Warmly promising a rumbling downpour of a Summer Storm

Sometime right around half thirty

Where stories are told just as colorfully as the rainbow that follows

On front porches with rocking chairs

Porches and chairs

As much a taken-for-granted part of the environment

As the smell of the fresh rain

Become emblems of a home so heavenly

To those who depart

Emblems of a land flowing with that milk and honey

Which drips from the words of those?

Who have chosen simple wisdom?

Grit, peace and acceptance

That unique acceptance void of apathy and rich in hope

Emanate seemingly from the red dirt its

Ode Of Riddle

As gigantic Everest-like conundrum
Mountains of both entrances to win,
Plough into downstream, the round
Woven around, faux-proved being -
Not of the prime mover a genesis
Strapped me at the back of tolling
In recluse like the holy Meccan hermit
And the Bethlehem dispatched evidence

Via the escutcheon I peep in my solitaire
As my eyes prowl to walk in tranquility,
The mind to ponder yonder the mystery
To the central bank, coast I glimpse
The foaming eventide ripples in motion
Waving as it quenches its hue less eyes,
Minstrels the silence praise of the high
What moans I wonder, a prove he be?

The welkin wears his garment of beauty
Bluish, the sun burps his glimmering rays,
Smiles his light from her widespread lips
Unto the world, and goal the cruel darkness
As the moon, galactic stars open their eyes
Come the dark for living souls to bath -
In their rays both the pure and filthy in macrocosm
If its nature ordained, who originated the nature?

Could a mere duo-played game of pleasure?
Mid thumping hearts, thighs hedonistic friction,
Tongue-twisting metamorphose into regeneration
With weak watery phlegm ejaculated skirts, trousers
Swelling of tummy end from filthy liquid to clothed
Blood and breathing fetus and flesh to bones?
If that be nature-caused, where comes the soul?
Who so much mighty would its emancipator be?
Where is the straight pathway to the holy dominion?
Shall my heart lead me through, not misled by nature?

Echoe Voices Of Mother Africa

In my heart I don't possess glorious moments.
On my countenance I express frown smiles
For amidst my progeny,
Greed has immersed creed
Envy becomes no privy
The way to glory is gloomy
And has become a path
That is sloppy and slippery
So, the trickle is patterned to a brook,
Wobbled and wrinkled leading to a tunnel that has no ending (Malcolm X Jr)

Wanting to say what I felt,
But I had no emotions anymore,
And my tongue was bonded with the palate,
So, my sayings remain in my heart,
Do I have a heart of stone?

That couldn't store any more stones,
The heavy heart was totally burdened,
By the words that were not said.

My lips were opening to the air,
But the air refused to interpret the sound,
And the moon became so darkened,
They told me not to say more on earth,
They didn't want to hear what I had,
Because it concerned them heartily,
They shut my mouth to the ground,
And the life seems helpless without sound.

We have ears but cannot hear,
The eyes are cursed with no vision,
Beautiful skin to feel but nothing is sensitive,
Cute lips that couldn't mutter the word,
We stared at the truth and destruction,
But our senses were like the leaf that was cut,
No sounds, no words, no sentences spoken,
Because our world preferred the horror silent.

The quietness is killing me,
My bricks are broken into pieces,
The building was falling onto the ground,
And the pillar couldn't stand on its position,
I was chained in a cave with no air,
The speakers were destroyed with the silence,
They kept me in a Coffin where I couldn't speak,
The priest said nothing on the funeral,
Because the silence is been preferred for the mute.

The dead only speaks once in their grave,
The odor produced by them stated it all,
All senses become sensitive in the dark room,
But the severe silence made if no pathway,
Because the living preferred the silence in the light,
And the sound was heard in the grave of the dark.

Men Don't Cry

At the heart of development lies a fundamental,

Commitment to improving the well-being of all human beings

Through the expansion of their social, civil, political,

Cultural and economic rights.

Yet our modern paradox remains a reality in

Which millions continue to live in impoverished conditions?

Within the presence of a surplus of global wealth and affluence

We strong and have a voice but society robbed us

They told us men don't cry so we hold back

They say to us you're a man

You can't be seen to cry

Be strong, don't cry

Please hold your tears back

You are strong and resistant, so don't fumble

At crock we off the bed
In the streets we hustle and bustle
Trying to make end meet all day all night
Rapid social and political changes,
Sometimes prompted by different financial crises,
Food insecurities, labor uncertainties, health crises
And natural disasters
Making a clear likely impact of people's demand for
Access, reach and quality of opportunity and services

Yet they told us men don't kneel
Their heart is synonym to rock and steel
They say we're stone cold and numb
Heartless beings that don't give a dam
Despite the lack of healthy and flourishing economy
That should offer us employment
And prospects for improving citizens lives
Thus, the deepening socio-economic crisis
We battle with that has continued to ravage societies
Has tension the situation at worst

With all these frustrations, pain and depressions
They continued robbing us

Men don't cry is what they have told us
Men don't cry is a lie that they have taught us
Men do cry is the truth they have hid from us
They have taught us to hold back what hurts inside
Just like that, they have robbed us the voice of our heart
Men don't do cry like a little child

The Undesired Child

Bastard they brand me with
The Philomena in the jungle and phoenix chirp
In the high-pitched tone underneath the shrubs
And at the peak of the giant African 'Iroko' tree
I sought to rest and contemplate
His beautiful songs in rhapsodic melodies
As the hawk squeaks, vulture hovers, squawks
Become horror and awful cries
No scientist proves cognizance of his bitterness
Shall he call it the end of designation of nature
Then, if so who the source of the nature be?

He's the son of no man born of many dads
His mother doesn't know which one
His friends and society call him a bastard
No respect, no value, and no honor he earns
No mercy no love he is show
No food no shelter for him

But there's a story behind this
It all started when mama was young
Immature and unaware
Her mother was a sickling
So, she had to make all the ends meet
Life became unbearable
Every day had struggles
No food with more bills
Mama also needed to take pills

With a sick mother to nurse and nurture
She had to find means to provide and protect
God blessed, she had a body so nice
So, she gave it out for a fair price

For a dollar she got laid and used
For a dollar she got paid and paint
For a dollar she bought pills and pull
For a dollar she bought food and paid bills
With no strings and stains attached
In the process she went down
Took in every man to provide

But to the cruelty of life
Comes the demise of her mama
To complicate her life
Living in the fast lane with no choice
She was put with a seed
A child of no man born of many dads
And she doesn't know which one
She's on her own again to provide

He grows up knowing many dads
His mother didn't know one man
His friends call him a bastard
A son of mama's many clients

He Don't Deserve Your Cry

You don't deserve to cry
You shouldn't shed tears for a gone guy
For he has decided from his heart
That he ought to live in truth
He is never yours from the start
In fact
You belong to the jewels of heaven's gifts
For you are an angel among men
Dressed in angelic beauty
With a heart of gold
Don't seal your heart with wax
No
Don't make it numb
Heal your heart
And believe there's love
Soon enough
Your own will come
The one that you truly deserve

You've cried

It's enough

Now wipe away those tears from your eyes

And put on that smile of gold

For your one true love will come bearing many gifts worth more than gold

In his heart he'll bring love

With feelings pure and true

And his actions reciprocating the language of his heart

Now wipe away those tears from your eyes

Don't cry for a gone guy

He is never yours from the start

But soon enough

Your love will surely come

The Art Of Smoking

Into Froggy prisoner of ash and flesh,
Frozen waves atop flooded towers
Land raining rats in burning Marrakesh

Mosquitos ring around my forehead,
Acid bleeds air into dark sleep,
Watery tongues paint the dead,
Golden mudslides kill to creep

"Might your husband run?" I ask the queen,
My underground visa shakes the skies.
"As hillbilly heroin marches upstream,
Brown bread crumbles silver eyes."

Puppet radios saddle a hairy flank,
Toothless teachers steer the donkey,
Folded lips voice the chemical stank,
Sleeveless children race a monkey

Letter To My Future Wife

In the morning if the sun refuses to shine
I will be there to guide you through the darkness

You, the love of my life
In the many years
Of being together
I have tested your love time and time again

If In the wee hours of the night
You feel lost, hold on to me
It is for you these words I pen
To thank you for being my lover, my friend
As the season's change
Our love changes with it
I will be committed to the promises made

We stand together joined in love
No matter the stumbling block in our way
You shower me with steadfast love every day

We bonded right from the start
You stirred emotions invisible
To the average Joe

How can I thank you for being my partner in life?
You illuminate my days, you are my warmth on the
Coldest of winter nights
You are my fantasy, my every heart's desire

I can only offer my fidelity and ever-lasting love for
all eternity
For it has been and is my vow to you

Poetry

Poetry is that rich, fertile soil of the soul
Into which every human desire, and hope take root
And spring to life.

Poetry is heart music...symphonies and concertos
Hymns and anthems.... expressing the swelling of the human breast

Poetry is feasting on the most sumptuous of fare
Enlivening hope, satisfaction and contentment

Poetry is falling in love...is children in your home...is achievement
Of dreams...is recognition for work well-done

Poetry is sunrise glow and sunset gold...moon pale and star bright...
Soft rains and frosted snow

Poetry is seascape, prairie grass, forest paths and mountains majestic

Poetry is the capstone of all great literature

Poetry, sometimes sadly, is that cemetery into which we memorialize

Things past recovery...things we must release but never surrender

Simply, and best.... poetry is love.

Finding Peace In A World Of Conflict

Finding peace in a world of conflict
Is like finding a black needle in the depth of the night
In a world of hungry monsters
Demons in human appearance
Biding the highest bid
On the surface they are like 'sheikhs' and priests
In the inner part they hold the darkest of secrets

My tongue is sticky tape
On the ridge of a curious mouth
Fleshy ridges I've
Known hide beneath
The glue, and my moans
Are words in oozing from?
A sprung tight jaw

There, down the dust trolled

Brown bell of a hill, is a well blink once
Blink again, you will see
Another hole, the one within, so deep
Full, brackish mud on hold, holed up
In stone, layers along ribs like rings
on an oak bony cobblestone is
Wet sandstone, porosity beneath
Blue skin and another night tiptoes
Near the borders, slips
Through the cracks

Where's the moon tonight?
Clouds race from the coast, silver cotton
In a bruised sky winds are a lost lust and
Whittle away until I see a sliver of a slit,
Hiding in the sphere, trying on a
Smile, a Luna's waning
Hello, gravity as savior

For The Gone

With proud thanks giving, a mother for her children,
> England mourns for her dead across the sea.
> Flesh of her flesh they are, spirit of her spirit,
> Fallen in the cause of the free.

Solemn the drums thrill; Death august and royal
> Sings sorrow up into immortal spheres,
> There is music in the midst of desolation
> And a glory that shines upon our tears.

They have gone with songs to the battle, they are young,
> Straight of limb, true of eye, steady and aglow.
> They were staunch to the end against odds uncounted;
> They fell with their faces to the foe.

They shall grow not old, as we that are left grow old:
Age shall not weary them, nor do the years condemn.

The Land Of Hidden Thoughts

At the going down of the sun and in the morning
We will remember them.

They mingle not with their laughing comrades again;
They sit no more at familiar tables of home;
They have no lot in our labor of the day-time;
They sleep beyond England's foam.

But where our desires are and our hopes profound,
Felt as a well-spring that is hidden from sight,
To the innermost heart of their own land they are known
As the stars are known to the Night;

As the stars that shall be bright when we are dust,
Moving in marches upon the heavenly plain;
As the stars that are starry in the time of our darkness,
To the end, to the end, they remain.

Black Widow

She cries tears of blood day and night,
Red river never runs dry,
Unimaginable horrors inflicted on her
Questions never answered to WHY?

Haunted by vile atrocities saturated
In relentless pain,
Horrid memories keep her shackled
Tightening the chain.
Shadows scream louder;
"You'll never be free no freedom will you gain!"

Unaware the shadows can't hurt her
Nothing tangible there,
But choked to believe the past is over
She remains in a cauldron of despair.

She drowns in nightmares

A helpless victim is all she knows,
Every second given to her abusers
Puffs of lasting peace and joy sadly goes.

But one day revelation will glow her eyes
The tormentors only own her past,
She'll throw off the shackles, walk free from hell's prison,
A new life begins at last!
And
She'll look in the mirror it reflects her priceless worth,
She'll smile as she sees her beauty
The clinging horror now slithers into earth.

A Morning Walk Along The Beach

Taking a lovely morning walk along the beach
While spending a few days at inverness
This walk has many grand features on its way
Get the winter clothing on, no need to fashion dress

We pass firstly 3 statutes - faith, hope, and charity
At a small boat by the sea shore
Owned by the nurse who saved lives then, many gave thanks

Many of nature's highlights may be seen nearby
Having some trees with a fountain at the side
Along with red squirrels, otters, herons, and bats
On this peninsula such delights on your ride

The river glides past the island on either side
it can be dangerous as its fast flows so deep

this is in middle between a couple of suspension bridges
these were built in 1828 still standing strong to keep

Walking over onto the island you'll find 'Nessie'
the wooden version that's motionless and still
then there's a small amphitheater so grand
where in the 50s summer dancing was the drill?

Coming back to the city on the west bank
Passing the RNI* chapel and Eden Court theatre
Which is a lovely mixture of old and new
St Andrews Cathedral then highlights the highest rank

In coming back along to the city look up high
Your eyes feast on the castle along the skyline
Well, a lovely way to spend a January morning
Strolling along the River Ness, a joy so very fine

Royal Northern Infirmary (hospital)

Phases Of Character

The softened wrinkles
Around your eyes
Draw me a roadmap
Taking me on a journey
Through country roads
Vibrant scenery with a
Few bumps along the way

Kiwi kissed eyes
Often laced in dew drops
Sculpt spring warmth
Carrying with sparkles
Chapters of trauma and
Crinkled pages of verses
Longing to be relived

Cheek bones spinning a
Silken scarlet flush

Softly over a beige leather
Nestling a warming glow
Celebrating life's triumphs
Thawing winter hardships

Dimples sit like speech marks
Over crescent moon lips
Soft rose defining character
Drawing me into midnight
Escaping darkness through
The compel of your glow

Village Play

Up before the rooster crows
In the darkness tippy toes
Quietly not to wake the rest
Gathering up our poles and nets

Pack the car up on the way
Stop to get some needed bait
Driving with the windows down
Backyard animal noises, all around

Birds are chirping singing songs
Cooing chattering hooting along
Excitement fills you up inside
To the lake we have arrived

With our gear we walk the path
Frogs and toads and lily pads
Come upon the perfect spot

Under a shade tree for when it gets hot

Slowly as the sun begins to rise
Golden amber blue filled skies
Sparkling glistening dancing light
Rippling water beautiful site

Bait our hooks and throw our lines
Fish are feeding morning time
No loud noises or you'll scare them off
Before you know it, you have one caught

Very carefully real him in
Expert swimmers they may win
Exhilarating when the line is tight
Pull and wind him in just right

With your family, friend, parent or love
Relaxing, sunning, cutting up
Spending a fun filled nature day
Intimate bonding stress free play

Invisible Quivering

Golden hour and cigarette ashes~
A filthy place filled with regrets
Bleeding charcoal flows on the road
Grey fungi grow on the wilted rose,

Broken sunglass reflects the dark figures
Fumes of death rushing through the streams
The skin is tattered, dripping ichor~
Stained eyes with bloodshot veins,

Rumbling ghost inside the hood
Wails and hide under the cracks
Poignant portraits tattooed on the sole
Aching feet with every step-in front,

Tremors inside the rib flickers pain
Squeezing thoughts rupture the brain
Intertwined grape vines creep~
Crushed wine drips through the eyes.

My Unborn Child

Remember, when you will be born,
Your hater will be emotionally torn
Of course, you will bring happiness to your mother,
But might not to any other
Someone will blame their fate,
Other side patriarchy will hate
You will be definitely considered as goddess,
But only on festivals, Oh my goodness!
Your parents will drive by what societies says,
Killing your all ambitions, you will be forced to silently stay
Poverty will be the biggest curse for you,
And you will be considered as a woe
A day will come which overhaul your life,
Puberty will hit, make you hate red on the knife
Maintaining menstrual hygiene will be a concern,
Grave pain and misery you will surely earn
Sophisticated custom will bar your entry into the temple,

You will no more equivalent to goddess, will be treated as untouchable

Money will be saved for marriage, taking your talent for granted,

One day you will give to someone, leaving you mere a puppet

Here women's patriarchy is not new,

Will never let you "you", the taunt of those interfering women's crew

Your suggestion and wish will be undervalued,

You will be left secluded and your worth will be questioned

But you need to stand for your right,

Taking obstacles as a challenge, you have to fight

Never allow anybody to make you feel you are nobody,

Be strong and make your weakness your Antibody

My dear, darkness of this new world will haunt you,

Remember, courageous ocean also forms from small drops of dew.

The Immotal Love

I seem to have loved you in numberless forms, numberless times…

In life after life, in age after age, forever.

My spellbound heart has made and remade the necklace of songs,

That you take as a gift, wear round your neck in your many forms,

In life after life, in age after age, forever.

Whenever I hear old chronicles of love, its age-old pain,

Its ancient tale of being apart or together.

As I stare on and on into the past, in the end you emerge,

Clad in the light of a pole-star piercing the darkness of time:

You become an image of what is remembered forever.

You and I have floated here on the stream that brings from the fount.

At the heart of time, love of one for another.

We have played alongside millions of lovers, shared in the same

Shy sweetness of meeting, the same distressful tears of farewell-

Old love but in shapes that renew and renew forever.

Today it is heaped at your feet, it has found its end in you

The love of all man's days both past and forever:

Universal joy, universal sorrow, universal life.

The memories of all loves merging with this one love of ours –

And the songs of every poet past and forever.

My Phoneminal Lady

You are the throbbing pulse
Beneath my milky skin
Surging hormones like a medical flush
Resplendent sun and luminous moon
Flowing, ebbing and pushing the
Tides within my body

A faded note; folded, creased
Scattered prose burned into eyes
Consumed and tattooed
On the inside of pale skin

Sprawling ferns in the shaded
Courtyard of my ribcage
Unrolling frond fingers spiraling
Grafting with their bony greenhouse
The sfumato lips behind me
Monalisa smile soft, textured kisses like

Erudite brushstrokes

I tuck you in the shadows
Between sternum and pericardium
A darkened space closest to me

From The Ruins

Far away from home, there is a silk cotton tree

That evolves the most beautiful flowers one has ever seen.

People from over great distances gathers there to gaze at

The natives of Nianija and travelers admit and swear its stunning beauty and non-fading unearthly enigma

There once was a valley, a valley on a hilltop on the outskirts of my village,

The center of appeal and reservoir of knowledge

There were warriors, standing proud with swords and shields,

There were men of knowledge and dignity, standing firm on justice

Great farming with promise of harmony in their eyes and beautiful young ladies of honest and modest

They surrounded the valley, stoically watching anyone who entered.

Listening to their prayers with their stone ears.

One frequent visitor is a woman with a distant far away gazes in her eyes.

One can almost imagine the heads of the statues turning as she passes,

Trying to get a glimpse of the snail smile on her lips.

As if walking on clouds she would float until she reaches the statue at the very end of the valley.

Smooth marble, just the right combination of strong angles and soft curves and a face that shone with unparalleled kindness.

If one had seen this statue with one's own eyes

One would have understood how a person could fall in love with it and that was exactly what had happened.

The woman who seems to walk through a dream came to visit her beloved every day, leaving small gifts of adoration at the unmoving feet.

Bundles of herbs, wooden carvings and more often not like those most beautiful flowers.

The joy that springs from this woman rippled through the village and anyone who visits, would speak of the people as the warmest and happiest they had ever met.

Africa In Shackles

Cursed at birth of anguish no dearth
For parents a liability, subject to partiality
Her studies are curtailed, her ambitions derailed
Childhood spent on household chores
Serving males one of her chores

Bound by chain, her childhood is slain!
Oh! The anguish, the pain...

After marriage another agony begins
Criticized endlessly, hurting words stings
Beaten by husband, living in fear
A busy life, eyes filled with tear
No house of her own, can't run away
Unemployment, illiteracy comes in her way

Bound by chain, she is endlessly slain!
Oh! The anguish, the pain...

Restrictions in dressing,
Restrictions in movements,
Restrictions in mannerisms,
Restrictions special rules and regulations...

Despite this, she is forcibly plundered
Her only sign of life, her body is devoured
Bound by chain, her body is slain
Oh! The anguish, the pain...

Men are superior, she has to obey their order
A rapist, a beater, are men superior?
Insensitive to feelings and tear, are men superior?

How is she inferior can anybody explain?
Why only on her are placed so many restrain?

By not keeping her in equal plane, humanity is slain
Oh women!
Break the shackles of chain!
Now onwards, the slayer must be slain!

Fight for your daughter's education
Teach her self-defense and protection
Teach your son's to feel and respect emotion

When our children we properly train
No woman will ever be

The Negro

I'm all electrodes hardwired to neurons.
Everything from my toes to my fingertips,
To the split ends of my hair, is galvanized.
I'm totally systemized
Ideologically programmed and westernized

I'm a story to unheard cognizance; I'm a riffle in a big lake.
I have learned the chatter of catcalls in the trees.
I have heeded the sluice grunting near.
In sun, I've set up myself.
I am not veritably stable right now.

The edges of my skin are on fire.
I can feel the fritters of anxiety pecking at my skin.
It's a nails-on-chalkboard feeling.
I am inside my head too much.
Each disaster is too close to me.
Each disaster originates from inside me.
I cannot find the words to explain; rather,

I try to conduct my wisdom to you by way of images.

You may have set up me out.

I cannot do this so nearly to dusk.

I do not want the long night ahead to be lonely.

Hear to the sound of my voice maybe you can acquaint me in.

I'm not myself for a moment.

Others I'm just fine.

It's in these nuances that I try to find myself.

I'm no way going to give in.

I'm just chaos of a beautiful mind.

Maybe it isn't too late to save me so soon.

Crumple up the words; they don't define me.

Rip up the paper into bitsy pieces so they can not fit back together.

I'm tired of trying to advise myself.

I'm tired of being myself.

Maybe I'll come someone differently in my time than on earth.

Maybe not.

Who am I, by the way?

Double-Faced

As I walked through the valley shadow of death
I traveled through the valley of the fallen kings
Beyond the White Mountains
To the north of the great seas of meteor
To the south of the Red Sea
Far beyond in magnitude
I roared and rose high from the high hills of Nianija
A riddle wrapped up in a mystery
The balance of the world must be restored!

I rode wild in will over exceeding darkness
The grandiosity of my prose rose
Turn fears into strength
And Strength into might
I led a battle I bought and won a victory I owned
As a knight in the night
I became the nightmare of my enemies

In the shrine, I stood and drank their blood in vain
out of rage

Intellectual fools dining in pools
Flowing through streams of blood of the innocent
Yet protected by a flawed system
They are scammers! Scamming and scanning the masses
Deputed to defend and fend laws to suit themselves.
The fascist! The fascist!
The Marxist! The communist!
The feminist! The capitalist!
All shit! Behind shadow propagandist

Does the truth shock you?
They're snitches, sellouts, destitute,
They hide and seek
With their disgruntled dirty tongues in their checks,
They're terrorists, extremists. Desperate narrow-minded beast dressed in bulbous gowns
Apocalypse at peak
The future remains bleak.

Drought

Abandoned hopes to die and rot;
To each their own deserted plot.
Where pastures late to harden slush
And souls who cursed the promised flood.
Climate change as the order of the day
Deforestation without afforestation

They say plants are life
We must protect them if we want to survive
Of burning huts and blistered skin,
Machetes, screams and godless din.
Of men gone mad out of the dust,
Out of the cracks in wrinkled crust.

Old vultures squabbling over bones
From charcoaled trees and scorching stones.
Their nights as cold as are the dead,
The light of day hung, dried and bled.

In life as those who in their graves,
Like mounds of humankind in hollow caves.
Leave flies to reap the salt from tears
'till brined in grief and hard borne fears.

And all the while the glowing sun;
Who'd gasp for death, your end of time come.
Who'd pray, who'd beg, who'd hope for rain
And all who would, they would in vain

My Grandmother

In the heart of the summer, schools are closed
In mind-still whispers,
I remember clouds of obscure countenance,
My childhood admiration,
Tracing lines of escaping success
Outside limits amusement looking for life;
Full of hopes and challenges
A hope for a better tomorrow
In the heart of the compound we play
Peace and togetherness, we are known
No ill feelings
No grudges
I am older now, an artist of word worlds,
Revolving around missing memories of sweet harmonies
I remember your arm,
Dripping from your bed of happiness and love,
Your daring wiggle and soft body, half way descending,

In silent whisper of our definitive parting
You brought me to this strange, wondrous place,
And in amazement,
I was confused by your concept of success,
But you were always
My grandmother.
For you are all I ever known

If I could travel the tempest of time
Tracing newer, true beginning,
I should meet you walking down our hills,
As still a young village lad,
knowing dream in forever's child
Following you to the rice fields
To the garden and the Lumos
long before the throes of darker misgivings
stole them from your vocabulary's stroke.
As we rest under the mango trees
Listening to your sweet melodies
And your eyes would visualize a wonder in me.
As wizardry speaks
To hold itself and never allow history obey the rules of ruin

You taught me about life and gave me a better future
You are in me as I am in you, for you are me, I am you

About the Author

Saidou DM Camara

Saidou DM Camara alias Gainako Peot is an actor, a poet, an author, a debater, a motivational quotes writer, a youth activist, a Pan Africanist and a motivational speaker.

Saidou hailed from a village called "Sare Janko" in Nianija District, Central River Region, North. Former Head Boy of "Jarumeh Koto Basic Cycle School" and Deputy Head Boy of "Brusubi Upper and Senior Secondary School."

Former President of the Press and Drama Association of the Brusubi Senior Secondary School. During his tenure as president, he trained and mentored students in the area of public speaking among which now, are journalist, lawyers and actors. Currently, pursuing his bachelors in Business

Administration at International Open University (IOU).
Site attendant at Kerr Batch Stone Circles.

Former Secretary General of The Business Administration Students Association, International Open University (IOU).

He currently serve as:
-Secretary General of Young Stars Movie Production.
- Financial Secretary of Nianija Writers And Public Speakers Association
- The country representative of Equal Trade Initiative The Gambia
-The country Director of the African Youth Wing The Gambian Chapter
-Chairperson of Council of African Youth Advocates (CAYA) Gambia Chapter
-The Vice President of Literary Success Club - The Gambia, one of Gambia's biggest literary organizations.

- Education and Research Minister of the Students Union International Open University (IOU) Saidou has been an outstanding student throughout his academic career. Graduating as the best student in his 6th grade. And equally won, at grade 9, the best S.E.S student, Best English language Student, Best P.H.E ,Best student of grade nine (9)A, and overall best graduating student in 2016. He won the awards for the best Business Management and History awards, and the most discipline graduating student in 2020.

He is a National Poetry Slam Finalist 2021 and have work on and featured in various movies among which were: WHO TO BLAME, THE TWIST, SHADOW OF OUR CULTURES MAMA GAMBIA etc including other short drama series. He is a current participant in the "Voice Of The Youths" VOTY competition. An Inter universities solution based competition, Representing his University among a Team of three.

www.ingramcontent.com/pod-product-compliance
Lightning Source LLC
LaVergne TN
LVHW041531070526
838199LV00046B/1621